EVOLUTION CITY MC

**We ride to rule.
We fight to survive.**

Copyright ©2026 NAT LOGAN, Bluff Creek Publishing LLC

Paperback ISBN: 978-1-956466-39-1

All rights reserved.

No portion of this book may be reproduced in any form without written permission from the publisher or author, except as permitted by U.S. copyright law. This book is entirely human generated. Writing is an art and the words come from my imagination. Any resemblance to real events, people or places are either a product of the author's imagination or used fictiously.

A Note from the Author

Thank you so much for picking up this book to try. When my friend Michelle Dups came to myself and another friend with the idea for Evolution City MC, I was so excited. I was still getting to write motorcycle club romance but with the addition of paranormal friends. Here, in this imaginary future world of 2050, you'll find dragons, other shifters and many other intriguing and amazing things.

As with any new venture, I have to get to know the world I'm writing in. Rex is me getting to know the characters of ECMC District 2 and his book is the prequel to the four novellas that release February 2027. I hope you enjoy this glimpse into Rex and Angelique's world. If you've read any of my other books, you might recognize a name or two as Rex and Angelique's timeline intersects with my other books.

I'm grateful you opened this book. I hope you enjoy it.

Love, Nat

CONTENTS

1. Chapter One — 1
2. Chapter Two — 13
3. Chapter Three — 25
4. Chapter Four — 33
5. Chapter Five — 43
6. Chapter Six — 51
7. Chapter Seven — 63
8. Chapter Eight — 73
9. Chapter Nine — 85
10. Chapter Ten — 95
11. Chapter Eleven — 105

12.	Chapter Twelve	113
13.	Bluff Creek Brotherhood MC	119
14.	Other Series	121
15.	Evolution City MC Districts	123

CHAPTER ONE

Angelique Mallet tugged her cloak tighter around her face. She walked beside her horse, because the ground was rocky. With the moonlight she was able to navigate but to be safe, she needed to walk.

Lightning had cost a large portion of her money, but she'd known having the horse would give her an edge. With her situation, she needed every advantage. She'd been sixteen when her family had wed her to Hugo, and so many nights she'd prayed for his death. He was a mean-spirited man who'd abused her for years.

She'd considered it a blessing when he'd died six months and three days ago. She rejoiced every day. Even before his death, she'd known she wasn't staying in France. Her father would consider her a bargaining chip. At thirty, she was still worth something to him.

She'd saved money and made plans. At first, she'd just known she was leaving but then, he started appearing in her dreams— calling to her. Visions of them together in the new world.

The morning after her husband was put in the ground, before her father's carriage arrived, she made her move. She'd traveled to the coast and paid one of the deckhands to sneak her on board for money. Once there, she'd used herbs and berries to change her dark hair to a gray. She rubbed some concoctions she'd made to make herself look older on her face and hands, and she'd gone by another name. If her father ever figured out what boat she left on, she wanted him to find a trail long gone dead from France to New France. She'd even waited to buy Lightning until she'd reached a trading post two days walk from the port she'd landed in. The walk had been hard, but she'd been able to hide at different times, so no other traveler spotted her.

When she'd bought Lightning, she'd worn layers of clothes to appear to have a larger frame, and since her tutor had required her to learn a couple different languages, she'd used English and mentioned idly in the conversation she was traveling to visit her aunt in a nearby village. The journey had been long, but she was beginning a new life. Last year, in 1649, she'd been dreading what abuse every day could bring.

The wind whipped higher, the howling sounding like an animal. She waited for the clouds to drift, until the moon's light was bright in the sky.

She should be getting close. There, just up the trail was the entrance to the cave she'd seen in her dreams. She'd had dreams from the time she was young. She wouldn't call herself a witch. She'd been raised in the church, but she'd always known there was something special about herself. Her mother had told her not to share any of her talents with her father, brothers or her husband. Angelique had followed her mother's directions. In her experience, the men she'd known couldn't be trusted with anything different.

She led the horse up the rocky path toward the entrance. With the way the trees grew on the mountainside, if she hadn't known where to look, she would never have found the entrance. As she approached, she stepped lightly. She wanted a chance to observe the cave before being caught unaware.

She tied the horse in the trees and crept closer. No light glowed from the cave, but it didn't mean it was unoccupied. She opened her satchel, taking one of the firesticks she'd made out. The small limb with rosemary, lavender and sage tied to it was perfect. She took her flint and struck it against her quartz stone, continuing until the sparks caught the herbs on fire. She lifted her torch and walked slowly to the small mouth of the cave. In her dreams, once inside the cave was huge. The small entrance was seven feet tall but only three feet wide. She held the torch out in front of her and examined everything the light revealed.

Walls reaching above her head by at least four feet were mottled by colored stones embedded in them, and the pretty stones reflected the light from her torch back at her.

She walked farther into the cave, observing the two openings toward one side. She stepped into the left one, following it until it opened into a room twice as big as the first cavern, and twice as tall. There weren't any stones in the walls here. She walked back to the first room and took a deep breath before traveling down the other opening. The tunnel warmed the farther she walked. This tunnel seemed longer than the last.

When the tunnel stopped, she gazed in awe at the revealed room. One side of the cave had a pool of water at least ten feet long and ten feet wide. Wisps of steam rose from the water. To the right of the pool was a crevice that opened from the wall. Water ran from it into a small bowl that seemed to have been carved from the wall itself. She slid her finger through it, and it was cool to the touch.

She walked back over near the pool with steam rising from the surface. Near here would be the perfect place to sleep, the heat would help her stay warm.

The room with the pool hadn't been in her dreams, but the front room had been. She made her way out of the cave and back to her horse. She'd bring the animal in and then set up some kind of warning system for the front of the cave. She wasn't sure if there were people nearby, but she wasn't taking chances. She needed to eat something then sleep. She was so tired and cold from the journey. She only hoped she'd interpreted her dreams correctly. She'd didn't relish a man having control over her again, but the dreams had become so prevalent that she couldn't ignore them.

She was older now and wiser. If this turned out badly, she could always poison him to save herself.

Rex flew over the area, trying to understand what was pulling him to this mountain. When he'd left England, all he'd wanted was to leave the pain. His parents and sister had been killed. He'd been wounded, but somehow survived. So many times in the last fifty years, he'd wondered why him?

He'd wandered the open countryside in Europe, fighting when he needed to expend his rage or expelling his rage in more enjoyable ways between a willing woman's thighs, but even that in the last ten years had ceased to appeal to him.

His heart skittered, then pounded. He almost fell out of the sky, because that had never happened before. He and his dragon were one entity, although two forms. What had happened? He focused and realized he'd let his cloak slip when his heart had done that strange thing. He cloaked himself again quickly, and flew toward the mountain that seemed to be drawing him to it.

As he flew closer, his heart throbbed harder in his chest. He circled the area he was drawn to, flying around the mountain, using his senses to search for danger.

When nothing came to him, he flew back toward where the pull was coming from. He landed, changing from dragon to man effortlessly. After 850 years, he would hope he could do it. He still remembered the awkward transitions he'd gone through while his dad tried to teach him. How many times had he landed and fallen flat on his face— half dragon, half man? Or taken a half hour to go through one transition only to immediately switch back?

Rex walked toward an area that seemed to glow. He stood in the cave entrance, sending his senses out. He breathed in a scent that had his cock hardening and his heart pounding as if he just came in a woman. *Mate* echoed in his mind.

Rex wanted to rush but he stayed in the entrance, checking the area once more with his senses. If he really was meeting his mate, he'd be needing time alone with her to slake his thirst and cement their bond. His dragon vision saw the line his mate had strung across the doorway. Someone less aware would have hit it, and it would have given her time to run. Seems his mate was smart.

He strode to the back of the room, instantly knowing she was waiting in the tunnel to the right, so he went left to check the area out. A large room Rex could already see was a kitchen area with a place for him to work. He could see their family living well here.

Making his way back to the main room, he walked over to the horse standing by the wall. The animal could sense his dragon, so he pulled out an oat cake he had left over from his travels. The animal lipped it, chewing but still watching him warily. That's okay. Eventually the animal would understand who was top of the food chain.

Rex stood in the entrance to the tunnel, breathing in the light scent of his mate drifting down the hall. The faint pink glow from the cavern she was in led him towards her. His cock was weeping behind his breeches, and he pressed his palm against it for a little relief.

"Wait your turn," he muttered, and wanted to slap his head. Was he actually talking to his cock?

Every beat of his heart told him to grab this woman and bury his cock as deep in her as he could, until he bathed her insides with his cum. Her scent was calling him, each step making the craving stronger.

He fought not to walk toward her and crash into the room. He stopped at the mouth of the tunnel where it opened into the cavern. The faint light was leading him to the small form lying to the left of the pool. He couldn't see anything about her. She was huddled under a fur.

He, on the other hand, found the room plenty warm as he removed his shirt, standing in his boots and breeches. He wasn't sure how to let her know he was here. The last thing he wanted to do was scare his mate, the woman who he would be bound to after tonight. And it would have to be tonight. There was no way he could fight the pull now that they were only feet apart.

He walked slowly toward her.

CHAPTER TWO

Angelique stirred as the most delicious smell filled her nostrils. A smoky, earthy smell that had her rolling over, her thighs clenching.

She wasn't sure what was happening, her belly ached for something. She opened her eyes, a faint glow drawing her eyes to the mouth of the tunnel. A tall, bearded man stood there, his dark eyes and hair matching the man who'd been appearing in her dreams.

But this time, she could see his bare chest, too. His skin stretched tautly over bulging muscles, a dusting of hair across his chest. Even though it wasn't proper, her eyes couldn't help but follow the muscles of his chest, down his stomach to where a trail of hair started at his belly button. Her eyes paused where it disappeared into his breeches.

She'd never seen a male so unclothed. The candle had always been blown out, and her husband had worn a bed shirt.

A sharp pain low in her belly and between her thighs had a whimper escaping her lips.

At her sound, he strode closer. His scent wrapped around her, filling her with longing. He was familiar, yet not. He knelt with his hand extended. His eyes blazing almost as if they were lit by an inner light.

He'd been in her dreams and called her here, and without considering any of the consequences, she took his hand. Heat traveled across her hand, up her arm and through her body— warming her instantly, and centering between her legs. A deep shudder had her grabbing her belly.

"Aww, my mate. I'm sorry for the pain, but our coupling will make the pain leave," his deep husky voice said, her nipples tightening at the sound.

Mate? What was he saying? She'd dreamed of him but had never heard the word 'mate'. But the pain was growing and morphing, becoming an ache that she couldn't ignore.

She allowed him to lift her, tugging her flush against him. His hand slid under her hair, tilting her head up— until his warm, full lips claimed hers. His beard rasping against her face.

Oh my! Her body was on fire. His lips deepened the warmth she'd felt, and a sent a flame zinging through her body. Her breasts felt heavy, and she needed *something*.

"It breaks my heart to hear you whimper, but it will feel good soon," he crooned.

His hands disposed of the clothing that had prevented them from touching skin to skin. At the first feel of his chest against her breasts as her hardened nipples touched his chest hair, she pushed closer. Touching him, his arms wrapped around her made the pain go away, leaving only an emptiness.

"Please," she moaned, not knowing why she craved his touch.

"My mate, it would be my greatest wish to please you," he said, his lips kissing her neck, traveling down to her breasts. When his lips captured one nipple while his fingers tantalized the other, she shuddered— his touch making her toes curl.

He'd said that word again, but she couldn't concentrate enough to pull her thoughts together. The only thing driving her was his touch, his touch made the ache better.

He lifted her in his arms, carrying her back to the pile of furs. He gently placed her there, standing to remove his boots and breeches.

Her eyes widened when his manhood was revealed— thick, veiny and weeping liquid. She licked her lips that longed to taste him and feel his manhood in her mouth. The girth worried her a little, but she throbbed between her legs. Whatever was happening, he was the only one who could help.

He knelt on the furs, his hands grasping her ankles and opening her thighs as she reached a hand to cover her most private place.

"Nay, mate, I'll know every inch of your body. I've waited a lifetime for this. Tell me my mate's name," he said, his hands and lips kissing and caressing each leg as he moved closer.

"Angelique," she said softly, trying to concentrate when all she cared about was the fire traveling through her.

"Aww, Angelique, I am blessed to have you," he said, his warm breath reaching her core. His touch there along with his incredible scent soaking into her skin had a wave crashing over her, sending fire shuddering through her body.

His hands running slowly over her body brought her back to herself. He was lying beside her, her head on his shoulder, his body pressed against hers. His manhood was still hard, weeping his essence against her stomach.

"I have you, mate," he whispered, his lips brushing her hair and kissing her forehead. He'd asked for her name but in the heat of the moment, she realized she'd never asked his. What type of woman was she to not know the name of the man she'd allowed these liberties with?

"What is your name?" she asked, trying to quell the anxiety but then his hand swept down her arm, her fears leaving at his touch.

"I am called Rex, mate, and I would very much like to make you mine," he said, his lips taking hers before trailing fire down her neck.

She moaned at his touch.

"I'll take that as a yes, mate," Rex said, moving between her legs. His fingers brushing her core had her sliding her legs wider to make room. His manhood breeched her opening, stretching her wide. She didn't think he'd fit but a warmth seemed to spurt inside her, sending heat along her channel until he glided in.

Rex smiled at her as he pulled out and then thrust back in, planting himself deeper with each thrust until she was full. She grabbed his shoulders as he started moving— heat, fire and warmth spreading through her building higher as Rex moved inside her.

"Let it take you, mate," Rex whispered as he tugged her nipple with his lips.

Angelique let the heat take her, meeting Rex thrust for thrust, needing to be as close as possible and have him deep inside her.

"Can't wait. My mate," he growled, his eyes glowing with a bright light. Heat bathed her insides as he jerked inside her, then she was shuddering as wave after wave of pleasure crashed over her. She was letting it take her as he said until a burning on her skin, low on her belly, drew her back. Pain lanced through her until she groaned.

"Relax, mate. It's our mate marks," he whispered, holding her tight against him.

She squirmed, trying to separate them to see the source of the pain. Maybe she had a tincture or salve that could make it stop.

He rolled over until she was on top of him, his hands once again sweeping over her, gliding from her shoulders to her hips and buttocks.

"Shh, it's okay. Let me hold you for a little while, and then I'll bring you pleasure again," he said.

Pleasure again. She'd loved it, but she wanted to know why her mound felt like it had been set on fire. Had something happened to her? She squirmed, trying to move away from him but his hard cock was still inside her, her legs on either side of his hips.

She pressed her hands against his chest. Maybe she could see if she sat up. He loosened his arms so she could reposition herself. It felt strange with his manhood still inside her, but she looked down.

For a second she thought this might be a dream, because there was no way that a marking could have appeared on her skin - and one of a mythical creature.

"What have you done to me?" she screeched, standing up and backing away.

Rex stood, holding his hands out. "Angelique, it's okay. They are the mating marks. Let me get a cloth, and I'll clean the seed from your thighs," he said, turning to find a small cloth and taking it to the pool.

Was he serious? He wanted to clean the seed from her thighs. What about the dark marking on her mound?

"Will the water wipe away this marking you've put on me?" she asked.

He snorted, then chuckled. "Nay, that tells everyone you're my mate," he replied.

Anger flashed through her at his callous disregard for her question. The cad kneeling at the edge of the pool provided the perfect target for her answer. She ran toward him, shoving with all her strength against his shoulders. He was caught unaware and the momentum shoved him forward, face first into the water. She stood there staring holes in his back, imagining knocking him down as soon as he got up.

He pulled himself out of the water, continuing to chuckle. "I'm guessing from that, you're not happy. I can tell you I hoped for a fiery mate to be by my side— maybe instead of Angelique, I should call you my Storm."

"Why are you laughing? How did this happen?" she shouted.

This man who had made her feel so much was maddening. Her dreams had called her here, but she couldn't even fathom what was happening.

"We're mates," he said.

"You keep saying that word like I'm supposed to know what that means. What are mates? And why are your eyes glowing as if lit by fire?" she asked.

He stared at her, not answering. He acted as if her questions stunned him.

"I thought you were maybe hiding your essence from me at first, which is why I couldn't feel your dragon. What are you?" he asked.

What was she? *Dragon?* Why was he talking gibberish?

"What do you mean what am I? I'm a woman. You appeared in my dreams after my husband died. I knew I had to leave France, so I followed the call. It couldn't be worse than what I'd lived through with him. When I found the cave from my dreams, I knew I was home but I don't understand why you're trying to trick me," she said, reaching for a fur to wrap around herself.

CHAPTER THREE

Rex watched his mate wrap the fur tightly around herself as a protection against him. He replayed everything he said, and if he could kick his own arse he would.

How fate had given him a human mate was a conundrum. They were so fragile.

He knew of only one way to convince her of his difference. This cavern was tall enough and wide enough for him to change. Hopefully it was the right decision.

"If you had dreams, then you know there are things outside the realm of our imaginations," he said, holding his hands up to show her he meant her no harm.

"True. I couldn't share my dreams with anyone, because they'd think I was evil. I'm not. I'm just more sensitive is what my mother always said," she answered.

"I am one of the others. I'd like to show you, if you're willing," he said.

He hoped this worked, because he wanted her comfortable before the rest of the mating bond hit. His essence bathing her insides had started it, and the markings had set the next step. Now her body and his were becoming bonded. He'd crave her and she'd crave him until the final step allowed them to talk in each other's minds and to have offspring.

She nodded, sitting down on the furs, wrapping some more around herself. He didn't believe she was cold. She was wrapping herself in them as a form of protection, which hurt his heart. He wanted to give her everything she'd ever dreamed of.

"Please don't be scared. I would rip out my heart before I harmed a hair on your head," he said, stepping back into the pool.

"My mate," he said, placing his hand on his heart before a shimmer surrounded him.

As he became his other half, he watched his mate. Her lips parted— not in fear, but in wonder. She leaned forward as she watched him change.

It didn't hurt, he and his dragon were one. It was like putting on a different set of clothes. He was still the man, he just had his dragon's strength, cunning and penchant for keeping treasures to himself, and his drive to keep all males away from Angelique would be higher when he was in dragon form.

As the change finished, Rex stared down at her. He knew what she saw; a large black dragon with gold eyes. The gold was what she'd called the light shining from his eyes. His dragon form was easily twenty feet tall, with a large wing span.

Since she seemed to be handling it well, he spread his wings partially. The cavern wasn't wide enough to spread them completely.

She stood up walking a little closer. "Can I touch you?"

He nodded, laying down until his head was on the ground. She walked closer, her hand reaching out to touch his scales as she brushed her hand against one.

"Oh, it's warm like you are," she said, stepping closer.

He'd never mate with her in dragon form because she wasn't a dragon, but her hand on him sent a wave of protectiveness through him. He needed to keep her safe, and he needed her to understand he wasn't a monster as some of the books portrayed them.

Her hand continued to touch his scales before she stepped back until she stood in front of him.

"Please change back," she said, walking over by the furs.

He nodded his head and willed the change, slipping back into his other form, the warm water against his calves as he waited to see what his mate was going to do.

She wiggled her finger at him to come closer.

He stepped onto the dry floor, walking toward her, his cock hardening as he came closer to his mate. Her sweet scent called to him, but he paused when he was standing in front of her, fighting himself to not touch her until she allowed it.

"I've never considered the things that might be real from legend, but if I can have dreams of the future, then you changing into a dragon can be real too. I don't know why my dreams led me here, but you standing here next to me— feels right. As if I'm finally home. I have a fierce need to have your manhood in my mouth. Will you let me?" she asked.

Would he let her? It would be his fondest wish, but he had to tell her everything.

"I will, but I need to share something with you first," he said.

She nodded.

"When you welcomed me into your body, it was the first step. When I released my essence into your body, it triggered the mate bond and the markings appeared. The next time you take my essence into you, it will cement the bond. We'll be mated for life. You'll be able to hear me in your head, and I'll be able to hear you. We'll also be able to have offspring. I have no doubts and want everything with you, but I will not lie to have you," he said.

Her hand reached out, grasping his cock. Her fingers sent fire up his shaft sending a shudder through him. His mate's hand was grasping him.

"If I'm yours then you're mine. I can't explain it, but I need this with you," she said.

CHAPTER FOUR

Rex carried water in the skin he'd filled over to their bed of furs. His mate was voracious. After she'd taken him into her mouth, he'd been overcome with the mating bond.

He'd heard the horse whinny a little bit ago. He was guessing it was morning. He and Angelique had come together so many times. They were well matched and from her changed scent, he could tell they'd created a life together. Human babies needed nine months in their mother's womb. With dragon and human matings, the babies could be laid as a dragon egg and took thirty-six months to hatch, or the babies could be carried in the mother's womb to be born in fifteen to eighteen months.

He hoped Angelique wanted to carry their child, because the thought of her rounded with his baby and her breasts full made him want to beat his chest.

She was beautiful with her smooth skin and lush dark hair. Her breasts with their darkened nipples called to him, but he wasn't going to mate with her again. The last time he'd slid inside her, she'd winced a little. He wasn't going to increase her soreness. He knelt beside her, lifting the skin to her lips to trickle water into her mouth. Her groan as her mouth latched onto the opening of the skin had him pressing his cock down. He should have gotten dressed; she was too much temptation right now.

"Umm, that feels so good. I was so thirsty," she said, opening her eyes and smiling at him.

He would live every day trying to make her smile. It warmed his heart. She sat up, scooting closer.

"What's next?" she asked.

"We make a home here and live our lives. You are my mate, my love, and even more than I ever thought I'd have," he said.

She chuckled. "Well, you did have to wait eight hundred and fifty years to find me," she said.

In between bouts of being inside her, they'd shared their stories. He wasn't sure why fate had decided she had to endure her first husband, but Rex was going to make sure that everything from now on was perfect.

"True, my mate," he growled, just to see her tremble.

A loud whinny came from the outer cave.

"Lightning sounds like she's done waiting on her breakfast," Angelique laughed.

"I'll feed her. Am I letting her graze outside, or do you have feed?" he asked.

"I have some feed left, but I think there's plenty for her to graze on out there," she said.

He dropped a kiss on her nose and walked over to slide on his breeches. He stuffed his cock down, holding the material closed as he laced them up.

Giggling had him turning to his mate.

"Have a problem fitting your manhood in your pants?" she teased, chuckling.

"It's a problem I plan on having for the rest of my life. How ever will I survive having a wife who hardens my cock?" he said, smiling at her.

The pretty blush on her cheeks had him knowing that she wasn't used to compliments. She would never doubt her worth with him.

He led the horse outside, tying her lead so she couldn't run away. He closed his eyes and breathed in the smells. Small animals, but no humans or large animals. He walked back into the outer chamber. Stepping closer to the wall, he examined the stones he'd barely noticed yesterday in his quest to find his mate.

He breathed deep. He had his treasure that he needed to move here. He'd never been drawn to stones, but these might change his mind. The glittery gold and silver were interesting, but the deep blue stones would look beautiful adorning his mate's body.

Angelique took the time while Rex was taking care of Lightning to clean off in the pool, the warm water caressing her skin as she held it in her cupped palms. The warm water was helping the chafing she had between her legs. and the muscles in her thighs that were screaming today.

She'd stood when Rex was gone because she wasn't sure she could walk without hobbling. She'd loved every minute of him being inside her, but she was sore today.

She also felt different, and she wondered if it was because of the mating. She was still a little surprised at herself with how quickly she'd accepted that he was a dragon. Once she'd got over him being an arse, she'd thought through her dreams and how he made her feel.

He was the man she was meant to be with. The fact that he was a dragon only made him more appealing. He could defend them and their children when they were blessed with them.

She'd used a tincture to keep from becoming pregnant by her previous husband, but she hadn't taken it in weeks. She wondered how dragon-human babies gestated. Would she carry him or her in her womb?

She cupped her belly, imagining herself rounded with Rex's baby. She wanted to carry the baby and experience it all for herself, and she hoped she'd get to.

"What are you thinking about, my Angel?" Rex asked.

Angelique turned toward her husband standing at the edge of the pool.

"I wondered if I'd get to carry your baby in my womb, or if dragon-human babies were born from eggs?" she asked.

He crooked his finger, urging her to come to the edge of the water.

Angelique made her way through the water until she was at the edge of the pool— the heat of Rex's body keeping her warm even though she was damp from the water. Rex slid a hand around her, grasping the flesh of her arse, and laying his other hand against her belly.

"You can choose. They can be born either way. Once you decide, we have a small ritual that is done," he said, his warm hand sending heat through her belly.

"When I get pregnant, can we do the ritual so I can carry our young in my womb?" she asked.

He stared in her eyes, his eyes glowing gold like his dragon eyes did.

You already carry our young. She heard in her mind. Her hand covered his. She was pregnant with a baby already. She'd always wanted a child or two, but not with her abusive husband.

I want to grow round with your babes and nurse them from my breast. She thought, and knew he'd heard.

If you're sure, we can say the words. If they are born from eggs, it takes thirty-six months. If born from your womb, it's longer than a human one and is usually fifteen to eighteen months.

She thought through having a longer pregnancy, but she didn't care. The eggs seemed so impersonal. She wanted to feel her babies kick and grow.

Say the words.

"You'll need to repeat them. The female is the only one who can choose for herself. Seed of my mate. Babe of my heart. You will be nourished by my body I vow," he said.

"Seed of my mate. Babe of my heart. You will be nourished by my body I vow," she said.

A warming in her womb and heat against her palm had her looking down. A golden light glowed from her belly, then faded away.

Her belly felt the same, but there was something different.

"Can you feel the babe's thoughts?" he asked.

"No, but my body fells a little different. Not bad, just different," she said.

He nodded and drew her against his body, his arms wrapping around her.

"I love you, my mate."

His deep, growly voice had her wanting to have him again, but she was so tired.

"I love you too," she said as he lifted her in his arms, tucking her into the furs.

"Sleep, my love. I'll watch over you and always keep you safe," he said.

Angelique smiled and drifted off.

CHAPTER FIVE

Angelique rubbed her back and moved toward the kitchen. In their eighteen months as mates, Rex had worked to make the cave their home. He'd dug farther into one of the caverns to add another space where they could store food and keep it cold. She'd also made him dig out another space when her dragon brought all his treasure to their home.

Rex was obsessed with making sure their treasure was enough to survive anything. Metals were his first love after her, with jewels following a close second. He'd made one of the blue stones into smaller ones and then used his dragon breath to heat the metal to pound into intricate chains. She'd had one that she'd worn around her neck and her belly until her belly had gotten so big.

She was ready to have this baby, because she hadn't been able to fly on Rex's back for ages. Once her belly had made her a little clumsy, he worried it would affect how she held onto him when he flew. She missed it.

Plus riding on his back, watching him use his dragon fire always made her hungry for her man.

She'd wondered how he could fly and stay hidden. After he explained about being able to cloak himself and his fire, she understood.

She walked to the chair Rex had made for her and sat down. The relief at having her belly resting on her lap and not having all the weight on her back was instantaneous. She sighed and leaned back. It was dark out. Rex had left early this morning and said he'd be back late. It was his last trip away before the baby came. She was close to when the baby could arrive, and Rex promised she wouldn't go through it alone.

He said he had a couple more things to pick up to make their home secure. She just wanted him here. Her back was aching, and the pains she'd felt intermittently for weeks seemed to be getting stronger today.

Lightning's whinny had her grabbing a knife off the counter. Rex usually yelled when he came in. She hoisted herself up, her belly making her wobble a little until she was steady.

"It's me," Rex's voice called from the cave entrance.

Normally his voice came from further inside, but he sounded like he was still at the entrance.

She lumbered that way. She no longer walked, she waddled or lumbered because she felt like the most ungainly woman ever. How did women do this more than once? She laid the knife down and held onto the wall of the tunnel as she walked.

Between her legs, a heavier pain was making it hard to walk. When she got to the main cavern, Rex had Lightning inside her indoor stall and fresh grasses on the ground. He was doing strange actions at the mouth of the cave. She waited until he waved some grasses and flowers he had that he placed on the floor of the cave.

When he turned toward her, his eyes widened and he ran toward her.

"Mate, the babe," he said, lifting her in his arms and carrying her toward their bedroom.

"What about the babe?" she asked.

"It's close," he said.

He carried her into the pool room and over to the bedroom they'd constructed. He laid her on the bed, helping her to prop against the furs.

He tugged her thighs apart, raising her dress, then grinning at what he saw as he pulled her dress over her head, dropping it beside the bed.

He settled between her thighs, holding her raised knees.

"Are you ready to meet our child?" he asked.

"How can it be time? I haven't had many pains," she asked as she moved her hips a little. She was definitely uncomfortable, but not the horrible pains other women had said they felt.

"I've been muting it through our bond since it started last night," he said.

"So it's time?" she asked as a wave of something went through her belly, tightening it.

"It is. Push and let's welcome our son to the world," he said. He slid his hands down to her thighs, pressing them wide and holding them up. She grasped her thighs and pushed as a pressure moved through her then seemed to slide out.

Rex lifted their son so she could see. "Welcome, Talon," he said, laying their son on her breasts after wiping him off. Talon cried, then settled once his head was against her heart. Rex moved between her legs again, then grabbed the cloths she'd made ready and covered the babe and her with them.

He kissed her and continued doing something while she held their son. Once he'd moved some of the bedding from between her legs to a bucket beside the bed, he laid beside her, pulling her into his arms.

"Well, what do you think?" he asked.

Tears filled her eyes. She was holding the child she'd dreamed of, and her man was holding her. She was exactly where she'd always wanted to be.

"I think I love you and Talon so much," she said, settling against him, drowsy now that her son was in her arms.

"I love you too. Thank you for giving me Talon," he said, his lips brushing her forehead.

She laid against him until Talon started mewling. Rex moved the cloth, and guided

Talon's mouth to her nipple. Her son latched on, suckling strongly.

Here in this mountain cavern with her son and her mate, she couldn't wish for anything more.

CHAPTER SIX

Rex walked into the entrance of their home. Six years ago, he, Talon now aged 100, and Titan, his youngest at 18, had redesigned their home to make it more hidden. They'd also added an outside cabin farther down the mountain, along with all sorts of barns to claim the land.

He was glad they'd had the forethought to do that, because things were brewing. The colonies were not happy with England. He'd seen things like this many times before and knew war was on the horizon.

On the bright side with war brewing, his mate would see the positive side of his treasure that continued to grow over the years. He'd added many items including skillets, pots and pans. He smiled inside when he thought about the two large cauldrons he'd liberated from an abandoned witch's home. The metals would come in handy for making weapons if needed. Talon and Titan had already said they wanted to serve if the country was fighting for its independence.

Unfortunately his Angelique would not be happy, and he guessed he would suffer the brunt of her ire. He could hear her words and considered turning back around. He'd never been a coward, but sometimes she was on a tear.

He'd wanted to take the boys hunting treasure later tonight anyway. They could get away and allow Angelique time to cool down.

"I understand wanting to serve, but there are so many things that could happen. As long as you promise to serve together, then I won't worry as much," Angelique said.

Rex stood in the doorway of the tunnel, listening to his family. She was pulling out the big guns talking about them worrying her.

She looked just as beautiful as the first day he had seen her in the cave. Their bonding had given her longer life and matched her aging to his. It wasn't a worry now because where they lived there weren't very many people.

At least with the boys serving together, Talon was old enough to be able to cloak himself and he'd been practicing extending it to another. Dragon saliva had healing properties that they could both utilize in case they were injured, but they had to be in dragon form to use it.

His boys needed to experience the world and adventure. Serving would let them see first-hand how war affected a country. It was coming soon, but Rex guessed he had a couple of years to train his boys.

"How is my mate today?" Rex asked because he decided if he was going to make his boys work tonight that he'd give them a little break now from their mother.

"I'm good, but I'm sure you know that. I tried to keep my anxiety down," she said.

He walked over, breathing deeply of her scent as he wrapped his arms around her.

"I did feel you muting, but you don't need to. The looming possibility of war is scary. It's why I'd like to take the boys out tonight. We'll work on Talon's cloaking of his brother and some other things," he whispered against her hair.

She chuckled and leaned her head back, her eyes glinting.

"Oh, you can say it's to teach the boys but we both know you're itching to add to your hoard. It's been a whole three weeks since you've brought something home," she said.

He nodded because his mate knew him too well. Something was telling him he needed to go treasure hunting in Europe. It was almost an itch at the back of his neck. He wasn't sure why he was being called there.

The last time he'd been called it was by his mate, but he was already mated.

"If you boys bring home any big items, you'll be spending the summer expanding the cave. I won't have your treasure crowding our space," she warned.

"Of course, I don't want anyone else to see and covet my hoard," Talon said, staring at his brother.

"What? I haven't touched your hoard. You're imagining things," Titan replied, sticking his tongue out.

They might be older, but they were still brothers that found every opportunity to fight. He still remembered the fight of 1765. Titan was twelve, and Talon had tackled him to the floor in the kitchen. Titan hadn't been working with his dragon self for long and his control was crap. He'd transformed in the kitchen, his body crushing the kitchen table and chairs. He'd been so shocked that he'd turned around, his tail sweeping across the food Angelique had been making.

After that fiasco, Angelique had put them to work making a large room where they all could be in dragon form without destroying anything.

"Stop. No fighting," Angelique said.

"Mom," they whined.

His wife's eyes blazed and her face would have scared him if her ire was directed at him. She glanced at the boys, slid her hand around his neck and pulled his lips to hers.

Her tongue slid across the seam of his lips, and he opened to let her lead.

"Eww, yuck. I don't want to see that," Talon whined.

"I think I'm going to be sick," Titan muttered.

His mate's hand slid between them to cup his cock through his breeches.

"Let's go. I can't watch this," Talon said.

Rex didn't care where they went because he was too interested in what his mate's fingers were doing to his cock.

Angelique waited until the boys left then pulled away.

"Mate, I'm irritated with our boys and want time alone with you," she said.

"What do you have in mind?" he asked

"Take me flying. It always relaxes me," she said. She loved flying with Rex. He could cloak them and fly high enough they wouldn't disturb or be seen by anyone on the ground. Not that there were many people close by.

She'd known that some day her children might need to fight, but it was hard to face. She couldn't imagine the fear a human woman who didn't have sons who had special powers dealt with.

Change was coming but with her mate, she knew they would be safer than most.

Rex led her outside, moving to the area that he had built where large trees made a natural hedge around a large area in the middle. He could transform and take off from there.

He walked toward her, smiled and changed. She stepped closer after he lay down with his head on the ground, rubbing her hands along his black scales as she went to the leg she used to mount. His gold eyes glowed as they followed her, and she crawled up to where she could ride him.

"Let's go," she said.

He stood up slowly and stretched his wings wide. A couple steps and he was soaring over the trees. The breeze rushed by her, but she had breeches under her dress and the heat of his dragon kept the parts of her touching him warm.

She watched the countryside as Rex flew them around their land and the surrounding area.

Although she'd kissed him and handled his cock to get the boys to leave, Rex had known when she asked for a flight that she wanted to talk without her sons around to hear.

Dragon hearing was great, and she clearly didn't want them to hear her fears. Rex flew around the area near a stream they liked to visit, and she waited while he made sure there weren't any predators that could hurt them.

He flew them down and landed, lying flat so she could move down his leg. She waited while he transformed. After he changed, he led her to the tree by the stream. He leaned against it, pulling her down between his legs. She relaxed against him.

"What do you need?" he asked.

Their bond gave him an advantage over other men. He could feel her unrest vibrating between them.

"I want you to tell me everything will be okay, but I don't want you to lie to me. The boys are more than I ever thought we'd have, and to let them go out into the world scares me to death," she poured out.

His lips brushed her head, his arms tightening to let her know he had her.

"I remember my mother when I left on my first excursion as a dragon. She was petrified. Back then, most dragons when they reached the maturity that they could cloak went on a solo trip for two weeks. She was so scared with all the unrest around us. My father who I consider a very wise man said these words to her and I think it might comfort both of us," he said.

She turned in his arms, because she wanted to see his face when he spoke.

"Our children are a gift that we get to shepherd while they are young. Once grown we must let them follow their own path, trusting we have taught them well. Even after all this time, I miss my father's wise words," Rex said, his eyes brimming with his love for her and their boys.

"Your father was a wise man who I wish I would have had the privilege to meet. He's right. We've taught them and shepherded them to know what they should do. What if them leaving eventually helps them find mates too?" she asked.

She breathed in deep of the crisp, clean air, hearing the birds in the trees. It would be hard to have the boys leave, but she'd never keep them from growing up.

"I thought they might help, and I worry about them too. We've taught them, but there are unscrupulous people in the world. We will continue equipping them as well as we can, and then wish them well when the time comes for them to leave," he said, turning her so she was cuddled on his lap.

"My mate, my love, we will always work through things together," he promised.

The promise he made shimmered through their bond, warming her from the inside. They would get through this together, and hopefully she'd have more time with her boys.

CHAPTER SEVEN

Rex flew through the air, dipping down on the air currents, his black dragon leading the way. Talon's dragon was a steel gray with pale pink edges on his scales. Titan's dragon was exactly the opposite of Talon's. His scales were a rose color with steel gray tips. Oh, the teasing that he'd had to listen to when Titan's dragon had been that color of pink.

When Talon wouldn't shut up and listen to their mother telling them to quiet down, Rex had imposed punishments on both the boys. He'd taken away Talon's ability to fly and turned both boys' scales the colors of rainbows.

Until then, neither boy had known that the head dragon of the clan could impose penalties. At least it had helped their attitudes for a little while.

Tonight, something was pulling him. He'd warned the boys before they left that he was feeling pulled toward Europe. Once they'd crossed the sea, he talked to the boys across the clan bond. Titan had only been able to hear them in the last year.

He'd asked them to tell him if they felt any type of pull. There were strange and wondrous things that humans knew nothing about. Rex couldn't tell if the pull was something natural, from another dragon in trouble, or if it was an artificial pull set as a trap for him.

He flew across the land until the faint smell of fire and smoke drifted by.

Keep alert.
Yes, Dad.
Yes, Dad.

He flew them closer to the increasingly strong smell of burnt wood and flesh. He crested a hill and saw the remains of a still smoldering castle.

Stay cloaked and land by the trees to the left. I'll take one pass over by myself.

Dad!

Do as I say. Stay hidden.

Rex waited until the boys landed and were settled. He flew up and circled the castle, keeping high to hopefully sense more information. He closed his eyes, opening himself to focus on his sense of hearing.

The fire still crackled in some places with quiet crack and pop sounds. The wind whistled as it blew through the remains. He picked up the scurry of some rodents that had escaped the blaze and were now searching for food or shelter. His heart thrummed as he passed over the remains of what he guessed were the dungeons where a faint cry seemed to come from the rubble. He focused on that area, and picked up two slow heartbeats. He checked for any humans besides his sons, and sensing no threats, called the boys to his location and landed. Switching back to human, once the boys were beside him, he asked the question that had been plaguing him.

"Am I crazy, or do you sense two faint heartbeats down there?" he asked.

"I hear them too," Talon said.

"Titan, shift and lift the heavy items. Talon and I will dig the delicate parts," Rex directed.

He and the boys started working, following the call that told him which way to dig. He held up his hand to stop Titan. Kneeling on the ground, he moved a large metal shield that was covering a metal box. Sliding it to the side, he stared.

He lifted the first small babe from the box, handing her to Talon. "Put her close to your skin and wrap the fur around her." Rex had never been happier that the magic of being a dragon allowed them to materialize clothes as they transformed if they wished.

Once he'd moved one girl, another one was revealed. Her sister had been almost completely covering her. At least he assumed they were sisters. He lifted the smaller girl out, cuddling her close. Breathing in her scent, he paused to breathe in the other girl's scent.

"Dad, they're dragons," Talon whispered.

"Yes, and full dragons because dragons and humans can rarely produce female dragons. The human has to have had something other in their family line," he said as he looked at what was left. How the girls survived was a mystery but as the cold wind picked up, he knew they needed to get moving.

"We're going to need something warmer for them, and a way to get them home."

"I saw a house that had clothing hanging outside about half an hour that way. How would we keep them on our dragons?" Talon asked.

"I'll fly. You two will stay human and hold the girls on my back. Let's see if somewhere has a good rope that we could weave something to keep you all there comfortably," Rex suggested.

Talon nodded, putting the girl he was holding up by his neck so her face was out of the wind.

In no time, he'd changed to his dragon form and the boys were riding him, holding the girls. They paused at the farmhouse and took some of the furs and clothes for the girls.

Rex couldn't leave them with nothing in exchange, so he parted with one of the jewels he'd found before they left the country.

They made the long flight back to home. Rex was thankful he'd carried more on his back over the years. Two adults and two children didn't even require him to make an extra stop for rest.

Once he'd landed and transformed, they headed to the entrance, where he spotted Angelique standing.

"Was something wrong? You usually don't come back until morning," she said.

Rex had considered sending word through their bond of what he'd found, but he'd deliberately hidden it. He wanted to see her face when he told her what treasure he'd found.

"I found what was calling me," he said.

"What was it?" she asked, staring at the bundles the boys carried.

Rex slid his arm around her, turning her toward the boys. "Our daughters were calling us. They're dragons, and their castle and the surrounding village had been burned down. I'm not sure how the girls survived, but they did," he said.

"Oh," Angelique said, reaching to pull the cloth back to see each girl's face.

"Bring them inside. They must be so tired and scared," she said.

In no time, his mate had the girls in warm clothes and having something to fill their bellies by the warm fire.

"Do they have names?" she asked, the happiness radiating from her bringing a smile to his face.

Rex knelt by his wife, his sons huddling close.

"They are named whatever you want to name your daughters," Rex said.

"Boys, any ideas?" she asked.

"Phoenix for this one, because she rose from the ashes of her house and called to Dad to find her," Talon said.

Angelique smiled and kissed the baby's cheek. "Oh, I like that. Welcome to the family Phoenix," she crooned.

"I think this one should be Dantea. She endured until we could rescue her," Titan said.

Rex smiled. Angelique was her own type of hoarder. She hoarded books and taught the boys to read and appreciate it. Seems she was a dragon after all with her treasure.

"Oh, that's beautiful. Welcome to the family Dantea," she crooned. His mate's beautiful smile and shining eyes caught his gaze.

Thank you! I love our family. She mouthed and sent a wash of love through their bond. He'd never get tired of feeling it wash over him.

CHAPTER EIGHT

Angelique stood in the kitchen of the cabin and breathed in the quiet. So many things had changed in the years since the girls had come to them. Talon and Titan served in the Revolutionary War and the war of 1812, and both came home safely.

Rex expanded their land as more and more people came to what became known first as Montana Territory, and then later as the state of Montana.

Beast, her next to youngest son had been born in 1850 and Barbarian, her youngest would be a year old in November this year. 1950 marked her and Rex's almost 300-year anniversary.

He'd planned a trip for them and said he was bringing home how they were going to go. She wasn't sure if he was buying them a bigger car or truck. She was just looking forward to spending some time with her husband without all the kids.

With more people and things coming to Montana, they'd had to become so much more careful with how they interacted with people. Rex missed being able to fly all the time but even cloaked, if the government had their radar trained the right way, Rex could appear. Sometimes if he knew it was there he could disrupt it, but they were just more careful now.

A loud, rumbling motor drew her attention outside. She put away the dish she'd been drying and walked to the door.

Her mate with the biggest smile on his face pulled up on one of those Harley Davidson motorcycles he and the boys had been discussing. It stood to reason with her husband's affinity for filling his treasury with metal items that they would end up owning motorcycles.

He pulled to a stop and shut off the engine.

"What do you think?" he asked, as all their children spilled out of the surrounding buildings.

"I think it puts a smile on your face, and if it makes us fly on the road then it sounds perfect," she said, leaning close to kiss his grinning mouth.

"Oh, Dad, I need one of these," Talon said.

"Well, about that. I think we should have a dealership. We can sell bikes retail for other brands and who knows, maybe with your abilities some of you might want to design and build motorcycles. I bought a property. Welcome to Black Dragon Customs. Would my mate like to take a ride?" he asked.

"Yes but..." she paused when he held up his hand. Reaching into the bags attached to the sides of the back wheel, he pulled out a pair of leather pants and a jacket.

"Change into these and wear your boots. I can't wait to have your arms wrapped around me," he said.

She ran back into the house and quickly changed. Her man had never led her wrong, and to be able to hold him and fly down the road sounded perfect.

She ran back out as if she was a young girl, but she felt young when she was with Rex.

He held out his hand and helped her cuddle up behind him, wrapping her arms around his waist. They were sharing one seat and if they would be going on a trip on this, she had some modifications that might need to be made.

He started the bike back up and the rumble between her thighs had her wondering if after their ride there was some place they could pull over. It had been hours since she and her mate had time alone.

Rex started slow but as soon as he knew she loved it, he sped up. It was just like when they were in the sky, the wind blowing in her hair, and her feeling as if she could do anything.

Rex drove them down the mountain, through a couple of turns until he could hit a road that was smoother.

They rode for hours, until night started to darken the sky. He headed back toward home, pulling to a stop about five miles from their house where he shut the engine down and helped her off.

"Growth is coming, and I'd rather be in charge of it. We could have motorcycle sales here with maybe a store that sold groceries and things people needed. With the cattle we raise and your vegetables, we're pretty self-sufficient but I'd like to work on protecting us a little more. What do you think?" he asked.

She turned and tugged his head down, their lips millimeters apart. "I think my dragon mate is taking care of all of us, and I love him deeply. Things have been changing fast, and I agree with you. We need to keep ourselves safe," she said, touching her lips to his.

The cool Montana air picked up as night fell. She'd learned over the years that there were more individuals with special traits. Two years ago, a bear shifter on the run had taken refuge on their land. Once he'd realized he was safe with them, he'd helped out around the area until he was ready to move on.

She did have one more thing she needed to talk to Rex about.

"I love our family, Rex," she said, not sure how to go on. They talked about everything, but she worried that what she had to say would upset him.

"I hear a but in there. What is bothering you my mate? Do I need to get ready for a visit from Storm?" he asked, a smile in his voice.

She chuckled. She freely admitted she had a temper, and sometimes she needed to voice her disapproval. When she did, her mate called her his Storm.

"No, but I don't want to hurt your feelings," she said.

"Is this what you've been hiding from our bond?" he asked, settling onto his bike, his legs straddling the cycle. He lifted her until she was facing him, her bottom on the gas tank, her thighs laying over his.

She nodded, looking down. She'd felt horrible hiding it from him.

Ic slid his hand to her neck, his hand grasping her hair to gently tilt her head back.

"What are you scared to share with me?" he asked, his eyes glittering with dragon fire.

"I love our children. I am so glad we had them, but my pregnancy with Barbarian was so hard. Not only did you have to mute the pains at birth, you had to mute other symptoms while I was pregnant," she said.

"Are you saying you want Barbarian to be our last offspring?" he asked.

She nodded.

"My love. I was so scared with how Barbarian seemed to be such a rougher pregnancy. I was trying to figure out how to ask you if he could be our last," Rex said.

She stared at her husband. She opened herself up and let go of the tight hold she'd had on the bond from keeping the secret. Rex's emotions about the birth and almost losing her washed over her. He wasn't just saying it. He was concerned too.

Tears filled her eyes. She'd spent weeks worrying when she could have just talked with her mate.

Over the years she'd learned all the dragon lore. She and her husband could perform the ritual at the next full moon. She didn't see herself changing her mind. She wanted time to enjoy her children and her husband.

"Now, is there anything else I can do to make my mate's life better?" he asked.

She grinned and sent the thoughts to him.

He chuckled.

"Mates for our children? Is that all of them, or since Barbarian is not quite one, can he wait awhile?" Rex asked.

She leaned toward him, her hand touching his chest then trailing down his shirt to his belt. Her fingers danced over his cock that was rapidly hardening.

"He can wait. Now, how about you show me how much you love me?" she asked.

He grinned the smile that promised her many pleasurable moments in her mate's arms.

She smiled at him while he divested them of their clothes, opening her thighs and setting about pleasing her. Despite years of making love, each time for her felt new and precious.

She groaned when he hit *that* spot with his fingers. "Oh, Rex," she moaned.

"Let go and enjoy," he whispered against her core, his tongue lashing her clit until she screamed at the ecstasy washing over her.

He moved and leaned back against the tree.

"Climb on," he directed, holding his weeping cock up for her.

Nope, she wanted to taste him. She crawled toward him, smiling when he couldn't take his eyes from her swaying breasts. She leaned close, breathing in his musky, smoky scent that called to her today as much as it did so many years ago.

The first swipe of her tongue had the fire moving through her as his essence hit her system. When she swallowed him, suckling strongly, her big strong dragon mate groaned her name, sliding his hands into her hair to direct her movements. She rubbed her hardened nipples against Rex's legs, knowing it would drive him wild.

"My mate, I'm going to spill in your mouth," he groaned.

She reached for his balls to fondle them as her lips locked around his cock, letting him know that's exactly what she wanted. He pulled her head up and when she swallowed him to the root again, he lost control. The hot splashes hit the back of her throat and she swallowed, the liquid warming her insides.

She licked him clean when they were finished and crawled back into his lap.

"Fuck, mate. I think you sucked every thought in my head out of my cock," he said, dropping a kiss against her forehead.

She shivered even though Rex was like her own personal heating blanket. A breeze had picked up and was bringing the smell of rain with it.

"Let's get you dressed and warmer. I'm glad we talked," he said.

She let Rex put her clothes back on. Him caring for her was one of the ways she loved seeing his soft side.

CHAPTER NINE

Rex watched his sons and daughters practicing defensive moves. Talon was pulling his punches when Dantea or Phoenix were his opponent.

Rex needed to get his point across, but he also needed his daughters to take a stand. Yesterday, the towers in New York had been hit by a terrorist plot. Although he and his kind stayed out of human politics, Rex had supernatural friends who worked together.

He had a feeling that in the coming years his kind wouldn't need to hide, because they'd have to take charge.

Besides the motorcycle custom building, they'd become a proper MC. It had been the perfect way to live outside the law, but also fit in. The small town he and his family had built had become home to humans and supernaturals who were willing to follow the MC's rules for the area.

His Storm used her knowledge of herbs and plants to build them a hydroponic growing area in their mountain. She grew some in outside greenhouses during the time she could in Montana, but they both agreed that they wanted to be self-sufficient.

It had taken him a couple years to remember to call her Storm once the motorcycle club was up and running, but now with the other members calling her it too, it was second nature.

"Oh, you asshole," Phoenix screamed, grabbing a large piece of metal and hurling it at her brother. Rex had dropped off some of his treasure last night instead of taking it to the cave, because he'd been tired. Well, he had to be happy that one of his girls was using anything at her disposal to fight with.

"You better watch your mouth, sissy. I'll be your President someday," Talon threatened.

Rex walked forward and stared at his children until he had their attention, "What's the fighting about?"

Phoenix stomped closer, crossing her arms. "He's not letting me learn."

Rex looked at Talon. His oldest shrugged his shoulders. "I'm just trying to protect her."

Rex motioned them closer. He stared at both of them until they fidgeted under his gaze.

"And that's good because when you take over the clan, you need to think about the safety of our family."

Before he could finish his thought, his oldest lightly pushed his sister's shoulder.

'See!" he crowed.

"I wasn't finished, Talon. Being a leader means you have to balance the safety of your family, the safety of the clan and how best it can work together. Sometimes the best way to protect them is to teach them how to fight and do what is needed to protect themselves and others. Things are changing— not today nor tomorrow, but in our lifetime. We can't afford to be unprepared."

Talon stared at his father, pursing his lips.

"I don't like it but in this instance, I'll bow to your wishes," Talon said.

Before Rex could form a reply to his son's insolent talk, his brothers took over.

Barbarian, Titan and Beast had Talon on the mat, holding his extremities immobile.

"You disrespected our MC President and the head of our clan. No one gets away with it— even the heir apparent. Right Phoenix?" Titan said.

Phoenix walked closer. "Hmm," she said, her finger tapping her cheek.

"What should his punishment be?" she asked.

"I know. How about he loses his ability to breathe fire?" Dantea said, walking in.

"Hey," Talon yelled, fighting his brothers to get loose.

"I'd say make his dragon have polka dots, but since we have to stay hidden that wouldn't be much fun," Barbarian said.

"Oh, if you took away his cloaking ability, then he wouldn't get to fly as a dragon for a while," Beast suggested.

Rex hid his smile behind his hand. He could almost see the cogs working in Talon's mind, cataloguing his siblings suggestions for when he was President of them. Maybe today would be a good learning opportunity for the future head of their clan and MC President.

"Let him up for a moment. I don't want this decision made under duress," Rex said.

The boys let Talon up. Talon walked over and stood in front of him.

"I'm sorry," he said.

"I know you are now. What I want to ask you is if you were head of the clan and the MC President and a younger member said those words to you, what penalty would you impose?" Rex asked.

His other children crowded close to wait on Talon's answer.

"Well, they'd be disrespecting both the clan and our MC. There would need to be a penalty for both. Losing dragon fire or cloaking for two weeks except in the case of attack on our compound should satisfy the clan. Cleaning the clubhouse toilets and fixing the meals for the same period of time should satisfy the MC," Talon said, his eyes clear with resolve.

"I agree. Your penalty suggestion is accepted and begins now. I've muted your dragon fire and cloaking for that time period unless there is danger to you or the clan," Rex said.

Placing his hand on his son's shoulder, he stared into Talon's eyes.

"You will make a fantastic leader. Now to be the leader you know you need to be, what else should you do?" Rex asked.

Talon breathed deep and turned to his sisters.

"Okay, we're going to practice takedowns. You both are going to do whatever you can to get me on the mat. You don't have to hold me there, just make me hit the mat lying down at some point. I'm not going to hold back, so prepare to have bruises. Beast, Barbarian- you're in charge of coaching them on how to take me down. Titan, you'll referee. Then we'll all rotate jobs. If something's coming, we're going to be prepared to fight," Talon said.

Rex felt a shiver go down his spine at Talon's words. He only hoped they had plenty of time to prepare. He stood there watching for a little bit until he felt the presence of his mate.

"Storm," he said, opening his arms for her to stand in front of him. Having her tight against him settled all the chaos.

"Did you set them to rights?" she asked.

"Did I not mute well through the bond?" he asked.

"You tried, but I'd been keeping an eye on them. It was only a matter of time until it blew up. I was hoping you'd be around because Talon listens better to you regarding women," she said, snuggling back against him.

Talon did listen better to him, but Talon was still farther along than how some of the humans treated women.

"I was thinking about having us fix a big supper tomorrow night and inviting all the neighbors. So many are in shock and scared. I think knowing we're all in this together might help, plus I was thinking we could have it in the clubhouse. I already have a dedicated helper," she said, giggling in his arms.

Rex chuckled. Oh, yes. His Storm would be teaching her own type of lesson. He'd guess she'd make sure that he and she dirtied every dish in the clubhouse, which would leave him washing the big pans far into the night. His mate had quite the talent for making sure a lesson hit home with the kids.

"I think it sounds perfect. Shall we leave our children to themselves and take a ride?" he asked.

"Yes, I could do with some wind therapy," she said, holding his hand and leading him out of the clubhouse.

She'd been wanting to take a ride on one of the motorcycles that they'd taken on trade in this week.

He swatted her ass as she walked away.

"Get a move on, woman. We're burning daylight, and I want a nice long ride with you," he teased as he headed toward the store.

After their ride, he might do a call with his allies and take their temperature on this situation. He hoped he was being overly dramatic, but he'd been through too many skirmishes and wars for control to minimize what he was seeing worldwide.

CHAPTER TEN

Rex took the turn to head them toward the Bluff Creek Brotherhood MC, Original Chapter. He and Storm had met Regina and Baron last year at the Sturgis motorcycle rally.

His Ol' Lady, Baron's Ol' Lady along with Rascal's Ol' Lady Meg and a few others had hit it off. Those women had relaxed and become instant friends.

Now that Talon had been President of the club for a few years, Rex and Storm had plenty of time to travel. He took the turn to the main street and looked for the sign for Regina's Roadside Refuge. They were all meeting there and then the ladies were having an evening at the club's coffee shop and bookstore, Broken Hearts Brewing. His wife was all excited because some author she adored was going to be there for questions and to sign books.

Baron had joked that they could mail whatever Storm bought that wouldn't fit on the bike. Wasn't that the truth? They'd already mailed packages from multiple places on their trip.

The ride from Montana to Kansas had been wonderful, but Rex was looking forward to a couple days hanging out with friends.

He backed the bike into one of the Bike Only spots in front of the café. Before Storm could even get off the bike, Regina, Meg and Hope came running out. His mate was off the bike and being surrounded by her friends. The volume of the voices got louder the more they talked.

He grinned watching them. These women had provided his mate a lifeline when she'd needed female friends. Their mountain and town had women, but not any his wife called close friends. Living for hundreds of years made it hard, but these ladies had pulled her in.

They had video calls each week discussing this or that about their families, the books they'd read or some strange item one of them had read.

Storm could also lament to these women about not having grandchildren even though Storm never could reveal that his kind had to find their fated mate. Which wasn't really the kids' fault.

"Well, seems like the ladies have Storm in hand and a full day planned. You ready to get a break from the bike?" Baron asked.

Rex got off the bike, accepting the hugs and backslaps from his friends.

"Yes, love riding but it's been awhile since we've done that long of a ride," Rex said, following Baron into the café.

"Let's get you something cool to drink and something to eat. Then we can chat about what you might like to do while you're here," Rascal said, going behind the counter and getting them drinks.

"And then you can tell us how Talon's doing taking over the MC. I love listening to the younger generation's screw ups," Locks said, chuckling.

Rex chuckled. "It's been a transition. Sometimes smooth, but his siblings have made it very rocky sometimes."

Laughter around the table had Rex sharing his contentment through the bond with his wife. The love she sent back had him glancing over to his mate sitting with her friends.

I love you, she mouthed.

Love you too, he mouthed back.

He turned back to the men to find them all staring at him with grins on their faces.

"A well-loved woman is a beautiful thing to see. How did we get so lucky?" Baron asked.

Rex wasn't sure why he'd been gifted such an amazing mate, but he was lucky. She was his greatest treasure.

Storm giggled at Regina's retelling of how she'd increased her herd of farm animals because of Baron continually needing to make it back into her good graces.

"I love that man, but sometimes they need to be reminded of the expectations we have for them," Regina said.

"Oh yes, Locks spent the first years of our marriage making it up to me for being a jerk. Lately, I'm thinking we might need to do a refresher course of what constitutes foreplay before the main event. Grabbing his dick through his tighty whities and saying do you want some of this in a Jersey Shore accent is not a turn on," Hope grumbled before laughing with all of them.

"Rascal has this mid-morning routine where he spends twenty minutes in the bathroom, reading the paper and pooping. Yesterday, he walked out of our hall bathroom, and he hadn't turned on the fan or used anything to dissipate the smell. It was rank because the man ate cheese and beans, which do not agree with his system. It wafts in as he walks in because the door is open now and in his sexy voice says, 'Babe, I've been thinking about you. How about you let me make your dreams come true.' Really? You've been thinking about my while you're pooping? That is so sexy," Meg says dryly.

Storm's stomach was going to ache from how much they were laughing.

"You know, ladies, we can whine about our men while perusing books and new book boyfriends. Let's head across the street," Regina said.

"Oh, I'd love to visit the bookstore. We don't have one close to us, and I have to rely on ordering. I wish I could just be on a list that sent me new releases every month," Storm said.

"Let's head over there, and I'll introduce you to Rachel. I bet she could set you up with some type of monthly subscription box. She has excellent taste in books, and I always read what she suggests," Regina said, standing up. Probably because they kept saying they were going across the street, then would start talking about another subject.

Storm walked over and kissed Rex's cheek. "I'm heading out with the girls. Have fun, but not so much that I have to curtail my fun to come bail you out."

Rex chuckled.

"Oh, we're good, Storm. If they do anything that needs medical help, they're to call Flick. If they do anything that increases the population at the compound, it better be because Baron is bringing me new animals. If they do anything to decrease the population, they'll need to cover it up themselves or establish dominance in jail until someone else comes to help them. I am not cutting my girlfriend time short because *someone* thought with his little head, not the big one," Regina said.

The laughter followed the women out. Storm breathed deep of the Kansas afternoon as warm sunshine with brewed coffee and sweets tickled her nose.

"Oh, she just got a whiff of those pastries Gunner was cooking. I want the cherry ones with the white icing— to die for. I don't care if my ass does get bigger. It's so worth it," Meg said.

Storm walked with the women, enjoying this time together. Becoming a motorcycle club was one of the best ideas her mate had had. She had friends who she adored.

CHAPTER ELEVEN

Talon stood in the clubhouse of his MC. He'd been President the last twenty-five years. He remembered how excited he'd been to take over from his Dad though he still relied heavily on his Dad's guidance. His Dad had thousands of years of experience. Talon was the oldest of his siblings at 398 years, but it was a small amount of time compared to his Dad's.

He'd just come back from meeting the heads of the paranormal MCs. He'd known they needed to do something about the state of the country and world. He was thankful that Zakeh from the gargoyles had stepped up with an idea.

He'd worried that when they all met there would be too much posturing in the room to accomplish anything. Sometimes the alphas all together could be a bit much. He'd been pleasantly surprised that everyone was as invested in the future as he was.

Now, he needed to get everyone in his MC on board. He didn't think it would be a problem. Rumblings from all over the country had them all planning and fortifying for years. This plan though, would require an expansion.

He'd called a meeting and everyone should be arriving. Talon walked into their meeting room. It was large, and the table was sturdy. Even in this form, he had some of his strength from his dragon form.

His sisters walked in and crowded close to him.

"You look like the weight of the world is on your shoulders," Dantea said.

Talon nodded. "On all our shoulders," he replied.

Dantea perked up. "Oh, does that mean we're going to be able to fly without cloaking and let them know we're here?" she asked, tilting her head.

Talon nodded, waiting to hear his sister's response to the change.

"I'm all for it if it means we have a way to keep everyone safe and get to fly unrestricted," Phoenix said.

"Oh, me too. Can you imagine the look on the face of that jackass who was smarting off about women in the bar last night if I changed to my dragon? I bet he'd piss his pants and run until his legs couldn't carry him," Dantea crowed.

"Is that something I need to address?" Talon said. He'd learned his sisters were strong fighters, but it didn't mean he wouldn't defend them if he saw something.

His sisters cackled then laughed so much that they were slapping their hands on the table.

"What happened?" Talon asked.

"Oh, I bet I know what you're talking about. Next time, warn a guy. I choked on my beer and sprayed it in the waitress's face," Barbarian said.

"Speak," Talon said, his power rolling through the room.

"Sheesh, calm down. No need to get bossy," Titan said as he and Beast walked in.

"I am sick and tired of jerks making their way into the bar, seeing a woman and deciding we're going back to cavemen time. He came on to me. I said no. He chose not to listen so instead of knocking him out of the front window on the bar which would cost us money, I chose to signal Spyte to enact the plan we'd talked about," Phoenix gasped out between bouts of laughter.

Talon wondered exactly what plan his sister and the skunk shifter had planned.

"Continue," Talon said.

Phoenix and Dantea kept starting to talk but before they could get words out, the laughter would continue.

"So, Spyte waddles in behind him, grasps onto his pants with her claws and crawls up his pants until she latches on to his crotch. She raises her tail, and he screams. Not just any scream, we're talking I'm being dismembered while I'm awake scream. He goes to pull her off with his hands and she bares her teeth at him and makes this weird sound. He lets go and screams *help me*, looking at everyone in the bar. Spyte lets go, drops to the floor, and waddles away toward the bathrooms. He turns and runs screaming out of the bar. It was awesome," Beast says, high-fiving Phoenix and Dantea.

Talon motioned everyone to take a seat. His mom and dad were the last ones in.

"I'm just going to say it, and then we can discuss. Zakeh called the twelve MC's together to give his recommendation to keep our parts of the world at least livable," Talon said, pausing.

When everyone kept quiet, he continued.

"We'll expand our territory. We'll oversee Montana and Idaho. We'll come under one MC— Evolution City MC, with our twelve individual MCs known as districts. We're district 2. We'll build a wall between us and anyone not part of Evolution MC. Within the wall, we'll be adding watch towers and spells to keep us safe. Thoughts before I go into it more?" Talon asked.

"So we're coming out into the open. Everyone will know about us. I think it might be the only way we have any lasting peace. I'm sure there'll be fighting, but some of the people might think twice when they see they're up against a dragon," Beast said.

Beast might be his youngest brother but besides being a beast when he fought, he also had a strategic mind.

"I think with the way things have gone that I'm going to have to admit that you all hoarding your treasures is going to be a big benefit, going forward," his mom huffed, crossing her arms.

Laughter echoed around the table. Times were serious, but it was time for them to take their place.

"Let me show you my thoughts on where we need the watch towers and who to put in charge of each building project, wall, spells and towers. I want your input," Talon said, rolling out the map of what was formerly the United States and would now be known as Evolution City MC. Talon showed the broken lines indicating the divisions between District 2 territory of Montana and Idaho and the surrounding territories. A solid line indicated where the wall would be built. He'd penciled in watch towers because he was positive his MC brothers and sisters would have suggestions of possible better places.

"If it's okay, I'll head up to the caves and take stock of our food and medicine stores. If we're adding Idaho into our territory, there are some areas that would be plentiful with some of the things we'll need," Storm said.

"Thanks, Mom," Talon said.

Without the need to hide, their familial relationships could be in the open without his parents, he and his siblings needing to reinvent their identities every hundred years.

They could do this. Because the world needed them to take the lead.

CHAPTER TWELVE

Talon stood by his bike at the front of the lines of bikes. Six weeks ago, he'd brought Zakeh's idea home to his MC. They'd accomplished a lot. The wall between their border and what was formerly Canada had been built, and been warded as extra protection. The watchtowers were complete.

Today, they were starting a two-week ride through District 2 to introduce themselves to the remaining humans and supernaturals in the district. But for the first time, their motorcycle club was accompanied by two dragons flying to scout for them two miles ahead.

Just because they'd claimed the land and renamed it as their district didn't mean that everyone was happy about it.

The bar and some of the businesses had been broken into as more people decided the downfall of civilization would be the perfect time to try to take what they didn't own from those they deemed weaker.

His town and the surrounding area already knew about his dragon because a week ago, he'd made an example of a rogue shifter and witch. They'd attacked during the night and killed the two oldest residents in their town.

Talon had chased them down. When he'd found out their reason for killing the couple, he decided to make an example of them.

He'd brought them in front of the clubhouse, holding them still by his power alone. He'd told those that gathered their crimes: killing two residents because the residents wouldn't say where to find children under five.

He'd let everyone know that he considered all the residents of his district as a part of his family, and *no one* touched his family.

He'd turned them to ash and didn't feel bad about it at all.

"All right, Beast. You, Dantea, Mom and Dad are in charge here. Phoenix and Barbarian, you'll fly for the first half. We'll rotate every time we stop and talk to people. I know this is going to be a transition but besides helping ourselves, we can help others. Our visitors let us know that our district needs to know who is in charge so we can keep the mayhem to a minimum," he said, getting on his bike.

The rumble of the engines filled the air.

"Let's see what District 2 has to say about our dragons. Evolution City MC, what say you?" he yelled over the engines.

"We ride to rule. We fight to survive," echoed from the people, shifters and dragons gathered.

He nodded to Phoenix and Barbarian to shift and take off. As they took to the sky, Talon waved his finger forward and accelerated.

Talon wondered what all they'd encounter on their trip and how everyone would handle seeing what the condition of their district was.

The pretty day was marred by smoke on the horizon, but Talon was certain that whatever District 2 encountered, they could handle.

And maybe Talon would be lucky enough to find a mate sometime soon. He was ready and willing for whatever amazing woman his was gifted with.

I hope you enjoyed this glimpse of my Dragons of Evolution City MC. I had a lot of fun writing Rex and Storm's story. If this is your first book by me and the Bluff Creek Brotherhood MC tempted you to want to read them, I've included where you can find them.

Regina and Baron's story is A Bluff Creek Christmas. Meg and Rascal's story is Rascal and takes place over the 80th Anniversary of D-Day. Hope and Locks story is found in Two Weddings and a Shoot Out. You can find them them on my website www.natloganauthor.com. If you want to chat books or have questions, you can find me in my group on Facebook Nat Logan's Bluff Creek Beauties.

BLUFF CREEK BROTHERHOOD MC

Bluff Creek Brotherhood MC, Original
A Bluff Creek Christmas
War
Bear
Scoop
Rascal
Roam
Cannon
Cruise
Slice
Two Weddings & a Shoot Out
Flick
Hot Cocoa, Mistletoe & The Road Captain
The Biker's Beloved

OTHER SERIES

Pit's Salvation, Saint's Outlaws MC
Justice's Reward, Saint's Outlaws MC
Tack's Bounty, Saint's Outlaws MC
Booker, Bluff Creek Brotherhood MC, Nomad
Twist's Raven, Bluff Creek Brotherhood MC, Nomad
Whiskey, Nelson's Honkytonk Saloon & Bar
Hennessy, Nelson's Honkytonk Saloon & Bar
Crewe, Nelson's Honkytonk Saloon & Bar
Halligan, Nelson's Honkytonk Saloon & Bar

EVOLUTION CITY MC DISTRICTS

Michelle Dups, District 1, release month 01/2027

Nat Logan, District 2, release month 2/2027

Cleo Browne, District 3, release month 3/2027

Lacy Rose, District 4, release month 4/2027

Mirrah McGee, District 7, release month 5/2027

Shaye Torrel, District 11, release month 6/2027

Renee Alan, District 8, release month 7/2027

Rebel Outlaw, District 9, release month 8/2027

S. Leigh, District 5, release month 9.2027

Kelly Lord, District 6, release month 10/2027
Ash Marah, District 12, release month 11/2027
D Williams, District 10, release month 12/2027

www.ingramcontent.com/pod-product-compliance
Ingram Content Group UK Ltd.
Pitfield, Milton Keynes, MK11 3LW, UK
UKHW020244240426
12048UKWH00026B/1589